HOME PLANET

VIC

SADDLEBACK
EDUCATIONAL PUBLISHING

red rhino b**OO**k s®

Body Switch	The Hero of	Racer
Clan Castles	Crow's Crossing	Sky Watchers
The Code	**Home Planet**	Standing by Emma
Fish Boy	I Am Underdog	Starstruck
Flyer	Killer Flood	Stolen Treasure
Fight School	Little Miss Miss	The Soldier
The Garden Troll	The Lost House	Too Many Dogs
Ghost Mountain	The Love Mints	Zombies!
The Gift	Out of Gas	Zuze and the Star

With more titles on the way …

SADDLEBACK
EDUCATIONAL PUBLISHING
www.sdlback.com

ISBN-13: 978-1-62250-966-9
ISBN-10: 1-62250-966-8
eBook: 978-1-63078-391-4

Printed in Guangzhou, China
NOR/0715/CA21501107

19 18 17 16 15   1 2 3 4 5

MEET THE

SAM

Age: 12

Hobby: astronomy, has his own telescope

Biggest Fear: doesn't like germs

Favorite Game: playing chess against the computer

Best Quality: adapts to change, but slowly

Linn

Age: 14

Big Secret: is afraid of snakes

Favorite Place: the Pacific Crest Trail

Career Goal: to open her own hiking tour company

Best Quality: would do anything for her family

1

NO SCHOOL

Sam stepped off the rolling walkway. He punched in the door code. His front door slid open. Sam stepped in and dropped his school bag. He clapped his hands.

"Last day," he said with a grin.

His dad was working at the desk. He turned off his vid screen. He looked at Sam.

"So, sixth grade's finally over?" he asked.

Sam nodded. "Yep. No school for four weeks. Yay!"

Sam walked to the cookbot. He punched in a code. It spit out a snack strip.

Cheese Doodlez

HIS FAVE
← SNACK
WAS OUT

His dad smiled.

"Nothing to do. No place to go," Sam said with a grin. He sat on the sofa with a thud. He chomped on the snack strip.

"Well," said Dad. "That's not really true."

Sam stopped eating. What was Dad going to say? Sam didn't want to work. He wanted a break. He frowned at his dad.

"You *do* have a place to go," said Dad. "If you want."

"What do you mean?" asked Sam. "Where?"

Dad grinned. "Your aunt and uncle called. They want you to visit."

Sam jumped up. His eyes were wide. Aunt Meg and Uncle Ed! They lived off planet. Sam had never been off planet. He'd been on short trips. Trips to other cities on his planet. But he'd never been off planet.

This would mean a long trip in space. His first long trip in space!

"They visited last year," said Dad. "Now they want you to visit them. They want you to visit for a week."

"What about Linn?" asked Sam. Linn was Sam's cousin. She was fourteen.

COUSIN
← LINN

"She's very excited," said Dad. "She wants to show you around."

Sam sat back down. This trip could be great. Or it could be awful. Would he like it? Or would it be bad?

"Wow," said Sam. "Wow. I really want to go. But it's a little scary. What if I don't like it there?"

"You'll love it," said Dad. "They live near where Mom grew up. It's a great place."

"When do I leave?" asked Sam.

"How about tomorrow?" asked Dad.

Sam rubbed his chin. He scratched his head. He looked at his dad.

"Okay," Sam finally said. "I'll do it. I'll go. It will be my first long trip in space. And it will be my first trip to Earth!"

SPACE TICKET

ECONOMY CLASS

Name: SAM
Date: JUNE 2032
Flight: QZAP3
Departs From: MOON BASE
Arrives To: EARTH

2

THE TRIP

Sam didn't really live on a planet. He lived on the moon. He'd been born on the moon. He'd grown up on the moon. But he knew about Earth. Earth was the home planet.

Mom and Dad were born on Earth. They grew up on Earth. But then they moved. They moved to the moon base. And Sam was born.

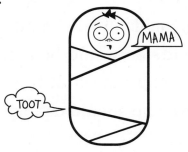

Mom came home from work. She was happy to hear the news.

"You will love Earth," said Mom. "You will love California. The fresh air! The blue sky! The mountains! The trees!"

Mom and Aunt Meg were sisters. They grew up in California.

"Go hiking with Linn," said Mom. "You'll see how great it is."

"I bet I'll love it," said Sam. But would he love it? He liked living on the moon. He liked living inside. Walls made him feel safe. Being outside would be strange. Blue skies would be strange. Tall trees would be strange. Maybe he should change his mind.

"I'll help you pack," said Mom. Sam looked at his mom. She was happy. Sam wanted his mom to be happy.

"Okay," he said. "Let's pack."

Soon Sam was packed. But that night he didn't sleep.

In the morning the family left. They went on the rolling walkways to the spaceport. The space trip would be long. It would take one day to get to Earth.

Sam waved goodbye to his parents. He got on the ship. He found his seat. He put on the seat belt. Then the ship took off.

Sam opened his pack. He had some flix

about Earth. He watched them. He ate some snacks. He watched more flix. At last Sam closed his eyes. He fell asleep.

A long time passed. Then Sam woke up. The ship was shaking. It was landing.

Sam got off the spaceship. He got on a rolling walkway. It carried him through the spaceport. Sam looked for his aunt and uncle.

"Sam!" called a voice. Sam looked around. There were Uncle Ed and Aunt Meg. Linn was there too. Sam waved. He stepped off the walkway. But then he stopped. He couldn't lift his feet. He had made it to Earth. But he couldn't walk!

3

EARTH

"It's the gravity," said Linn. "The moon base has gravity. But it's not quite the same. You'll get used to this gravity soon."

"We'll take your bags," said Aunt Meg.

"This way to the auto-car," said Uncle Ed. He took Sam's arm. He helped Sam walk. At first Sam dragged his feet. But soon he was walking fine.

"I'm okay now," said Sam. "I can walk."

Uncle Ed let go of Sam's arm. They walked through the spaceport. Soon they got to the auto-car. It was parked in the charging lot. Uncle Ed helped Sam put his bags in the car.

The auto-car drove itself. It drove out of the charging lot. It went out into the sunshine. It went into the city.

Sam put his hand up. He touched the roof of the car. He was glad there was a roof. He touched the windows. He was glad they were closed. He felt safe. Sam looked out.

"Everything is so big," said Sam. "It's so bright. It's so busy." Sam looked everywhere. He had many questions. "There are a lot of people. How do you learn all their names? There are so many cars. Do they ever crash? The buildings are so high! What do people do in there?" he asked. "There are trees growing next to the street. Who takes care of them?"

"So many questions!" Linn said, laughing. "I'll try to answer them."

Soon they were home. The auto-car parked in the garage. Sam was glad they were there. He wanted to go hiking.

"Come on," said Linn. She got out of the auto-car. "I'll show you around." She grabbed Sam's bags.

Sam followed her.

"Here's your room," she said. She put the bags down. She kept walking. "Here's my room. Here's the kitchen."

CLAIRE, THE COOKBOT

Linn showed everything to Sam. Her home looked like his home. There was a cookbot. There was a sonic station. There were vid screens. Lots of vid screens. Why did Linn's home have so many? There were vid screens in every room. Sam's home only had two.

Finally they got to the living room. Linn sat on the couch. Sam walked up to a wall.

"This is a really big vid screen. What a great picture of a mountain. There are so many trees. And what big clouds," said Sam. "We have a screen like this at my school. My teacher likes to look at the sea. She shows us fish and—"

Linn grinned. She stood beside Sam. She

reached out and pushed a button. Sam saw the vid screen move. Then he knew he'd made a mistake. This wasn't a big vid screen. This picture was real. The mountain was real. The trees were real. Linn had just opened a real window. Sam gasped for air!

Linn looked at Sam.

"There is air," she said.

Sam stopped gasping. He nodded.

"I forgot," he said. "I'm used to the moon." Sam looked around the room. "Are these all windows?" he asked.

"Yes," said Linn. "We don't need vid

screens. We have the real world." Linn looked at Sam. "Is it scary for you?"

#1 PLACE → ON THE MOON

← PLANT DOME

"It's different. That's all. I've seen flix. I know about birds. And mountains. And clouds. We learn about Earth at school. We even have a plant dome," Sam said. "It's the best place on the moon. It has trees and flowers. But it's small. Everything here is big. It's *very* big."

"You'll get used to it," said Linn. "What do you want to do?"

Sam looked at her. "Go hiking," he said.

"Won't that be hard?" asked Linn.

It would be hard to go outside. But Sam wanted to like Earth. He wanted to have fun.

"I want to do it," he said.

Aunt Meg came in. She looked at Sam. "Ed and I are going to work," she said. "But Linn will help you have fun." Aunt Meg looked at Linn. "Give Sam a good time."

"We're going hiking," said Linn. "Up the mountain."

"That's too much," said Aunt Meg. "Take a short walk first."

Linn looked sad. Aunt Meg frowned.

"Okay," said Linn. "A short walk. Come on, Sam." Linn went to the back door. She opened it. "Your first walk outside."

Sam walked to the door. He looked out. He sniffed the air. He looked at the trees. Then he saw something move. It was an

animal. A big animal. It had long black fur.
Its mouth was open. It had sharp teeth. It
was running. It was running at Sam. Sam
yelled. The animal jumped on him.

"Help me!" yelled Sam.

4

THE WALK

"Barker! No!" yelled Linn.

"Help me!" Sam yelled again. "It's eating me!"

"She's licking you," said Linn with a laugh. "Barker, come." The big dog looked at Linn. She wagged her tail.

I LIKE TO LICK.

AND BARK!

"Back outside," ordered Linn. She pushed Barker out the door.

Sam nodded his head. He watched Barker go out. He stood up.

"I'm sorry," said Linn. "Barker won't hurt you. She's a sweet dog. But she does like to lick."

"Was that a dog?" asked Sam. "It was so big." He wiped wet slobber off his face. "Why do you have a dog?"

"We like dogs," said Linn. "We got her a few months ago. Barker and I go hiking."

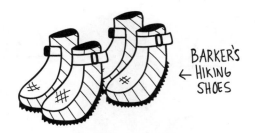

BARKER'S
← HIKING
SHOES

"There are no dogs on the moon," said Sam. "There are no animals at all. Except for some lab mice. I'm not sure I like dogs."

"Dogs are fun," said Linn. "But Barker is big. We'll leave Barker at home. Let's go out the front door."

Sam nodded. "That's a good idea," he said.

Linn went out the front door. Sam followed. He looked for Barker. But the dog was in the backyard. Sam looked at Linn. She was walking on the grass. Sam stopped walking.

"Where are you going?" asked Sam.

"To the woods," said Linn. "What's wrong?"

"You're walking on dirt," said Sam. "Dirt is full of germs."

Linn shook her head.

"Earth is made of dirt," she said. She walked on. Sam waited for a bit. Then he followed Linn. He walked on his tiptoes.

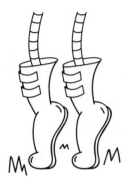

Soon they were in the shade. Sam looked around. He saw lots of trees. They were very tall.

"The trees are so tall," said Sam. "Won't they fall down?"

"They won't fall down," said Linn.

But Sam moved away from the tall trees. Two birds flew up. A frog hopped in the grass. Sam ducked his head. "There are so many animals," he said.

"They live here too," said Linn. She kept walking.

"The wind is blowing my hair," said Sam.

"That's what wind does," said Linn.

They kept walking. Sam was hot. He wiped his face. "Why is it so hot?" he asked. He wasn't happy.

Linn looked at Sam. "It's summer," she said. "Summer on Earth is hot."

"I know," said Sam. "But can't they make it cooler."

Linn shook her head. She kept walking.

Sam was tired. He was sweaty. His toes hurt. He was not having fun.

"I want to go back inside," he said.

Linn looked at Sam. She looked sad.

"Okay," she said. "But tomorrow we'll go out again. You'll like it more. Okay?"

Sam didn't want to go out again. But he nodded.

The next day Linn took Sam to a park. The day after they went to a creek. Sam still did not have fun. The walks were too long. And he had lots of questions.

"Why are there ants on the ground? Who put rocks on the path? Who picks up the leaves? Who feeds the animals?"

Linn did not like the questions. They were hard to answer.

On day four they were in the woods. Sam looked up.

"Why are the leaves moving?" he asked. "Why are the clouds gray?"

FEELING
ANNOYED

"Too many questions!" said Linn. Her voice was loud. "No more talking."

Sam was quiet. But then something new happened. It got very dark.

"What's going on?" asked Sam. He looked up. The sun was gone. Then something hit his face. It was water. Lots of water. What was happening?

"Help!" said Sam. "We're going to drown!" Sam began to run through the trees.

5

THE FIGHT

Sam ran fast. He was scared. Was he going the right way? Would he make it to the house? His clothes were getting wet. Would Aunt Meg be mad?

"Stop!" called a voice. "Stop running!" It was Linn.

Sam slowed down.

"You're going to trip," Linn called.

She ran up to Sam. She grabbed his shirt. She made him stop running.

"What's the matter?" she panted. "Why are you running? It's only a summer shower."

"A what?" asked Sam. He was panting too. He bent over and put his hands on his knees.

"A rain shower," said Linn. "Look. It's over." She pointed at the sky.

Sam looked up. The rain had stopped. The clouds were moving away. The sun began to shine. There was a small rainbow.

"That was rain?" asked Sam. "I know about rain. But there was so much water."

"That was rain," said Linn. "Look at the rainbow."

"Our clothes are wet," said Sam. He didn't look at the rainbow. He was too upset. "Don't people on Earth get mad? Why didn't someone tell us?"

Linn frowned at him. "Don't be silly," she said. "You'll be dry soon. No one minds a little water. Anyway, rain is good. It makes everything grow."

"I don't like rain," said Sam. He stomped off. He could see the house.

Linn put her hands on her hips. "Be glad this was only a shower," she yelled. "Sometimes we have big rainstorms. And snowstorms. Even hail."

"That's crazy," yelled Sam. "How can you live here?"

"I like it," yelled Linn. "Different weather makes life more fun."

Sam frowned. He started to talk. But he

bumped up against a tree. Water dripped down on him. It ran down his neck.

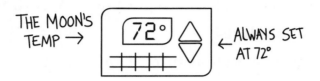

THE MOON'S TEMP → 72° ← ALWAYS SET AT 72°

"Ugh," said Sam. He shook his shirt. "The moon is much better. It's always good weather. Earth is a bad place to live."

"It is not," said Linn. Her voice got louder. "The moon is fake. There's nothing real on the moon. No water. No air. No life. How can you live on the moon?"

Sam glared at Linn.

"I wish I'd never come here!" he yelled.

"That's because you're scared of everything," yelled Linn. "I can't even bring Barker on our walks." She ran past Sam to the house.

"Ahhh!" yelled Sam. But he wasn't yelling at Linn. He was yelling because he felt pain. Something sharp had pinched him. He had a big red spot on his arm. Earth was getting worse and worse.

6

THE IDEA

Linn looked at Sam. She saw the bump on his arm.

"Sheesh!" said Linn. "It's only a bugbite. You are a big baby!" Linn shook her head. She punched in the door code. She went inside.

"A bug?" asked Sam. "You have bugs that bite? You let them fly around? Earth is crazy!"

ON THE MOON → NO BUGS ALLOWED... EVER

Sam stomped in after Linn. Aunt Meg was there. She looked at the two mad faces.

AUNT MEG'S CONCERNED LOOK

"What's wrong?" asked Aunt Meg.

Linn frowned. "Nothing," said Linn. She left the room.

Aunt Meg looked at Sam. His face was red. He was sweating. He was panting. He was rubbing his arm.

"I hate it here," said Sam. "I want to go home."

"Linn should not have yelled," said Aunt Meg.

"It's not Linn," said Sam. "It's the dirt. It's the wind. It's the rain. It's the bugs. It's all bad. I want to go home."

Aunt Meg looked sad. "I'm sorry you're unhappy," she said. "We wanted you to have fun. We wanted you to like Earth. Your visit is over soon. Only two more days."

Sam sat on the couch. He wiped his face. He rubbed his arm.

"Stay inside," said Aunt Meg. "No more walks. Watch a flix. Spend your last two days inside."

↓ THEY HAVE AN **EPIC** FLIX COLLECTION ↓

Sam nodded. He would do that.

"It is hard," said Aunt Meg. "Getting used to Earth is hard. Not everyone can do it." She smiled at Sam. Then she left.

Sam sat on the couch. He was still mad. He was mad at Linn. He was mad at Earth. Why was it hard for him? Why couldn't he have fun? Why couldn't he like Earth?

Soon it was dinnertime. Everyone was quiet. Linn didn't talk. Sam didn't talk.

After dinner the kids went to their rooms. Sam thought about his mom. He wanted her to be happy. He wanted her to be proud. He also thought about Linn. She liked living on Earth. She wasn't scared. Sam fell asleep.

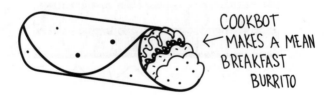

COOKBOT
← MAKES A MEAN BREAKFAST BURRITO

The next morning Sam had a brave idea. He went to breakfast. Everyone was eating. Linn looked up at Sam.

"I'm sorry I yelled," she said.

Sam sat down at the table. "Me too."

Aunt Meg and Uncle Ed nodded.

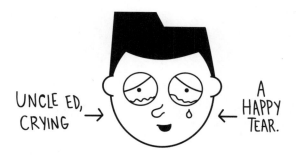

UNCLE ED, CRYING → ← A HAPPY TEAR.

Then Sam looked at Linn. He took a deep breath. It was time for his idea.

"Linn," he said. "I want to go on a hike. A real hike. Up the mountain."

Linn looked at Sam. She opened her eyes wide.

"Are you sure, Sam?" asked Aunt Meg. "Think about yesterday."

"Yes," said Sam. "I'm sure. I want to hike the mountain."

Linn looked at her mom. Aunt Meg nodded. Then Linn grinned at Sam.

"Okay," said Linn. "We'll hike the mountain."

7

THE HIKE

Linn jumped up. She left the room. Then she came back. She had two packs.

"We'll need food," said Linn. "And water." Linn began filling the packs. She put in lots of things. She looked happy.

Sam was not happy. His idea seemed good before. Now he didn't think so.

"Can we take Barker this time?" asked Linn.

"I would like Barker to stay home," said Sam.

Linn looked at her mom.

"Leave Barker home," said Aunt Meg. "You can hike with her later. After Sam goes home."

Linn nodded.

"Where are we going?" asked Sam.

"Blue Lake," said Linn. "It's a short hike. One hour up. One hour down. It's really cool."

"Is it high?" asked Sam. Would he be okay up high?

"Yes," said Linn. "It's on the mountain."

"Lots of trees?" asked Sam. Would he be okay with lots of trees?

"Yes," said Linn. "Lots of trees!"

"How do we get there?" asked Sam. He did not like auto-car trips.

"We'll take the auto-car," said Linn. "It drives by itself. We won't need Mom or Dad."

Sam didn't feel brave anymore. An auto-car trip. A high mountain. Lots of trees. His hiking idea was bad. But it was too late now. He couldn't back out.

Sam thought about tomorrow. Tomorrow was his trip home. That was a good thing. This hike would be the last hard thing. He could do it. He had to do it.

"I'm ready," said Linn. She grabbed the

packs. "Bye, Mom. Come on, Sam." She went into the garage.

Sam gulped. "Bye, Aunt Meg," he said. He went after Linn.

The auto-car drove by itself. It took them to the mountain. It parked in the charging lot. Linn jumped out. She got the packs.

Sam took a deep breath. He got out of the car. He tipped his head back. He looked at the mountain. It looked very big to Sam. He had never climbed so high.

Linn put on her pack. She gave the other one to Sam. She grinned at him.

"Let's go," she said.

8

THE MOUNTAIN

Sam and Linn began the hike. It was a warm day. The sun was shining. At first Sam kept his head down. He watched Linn's feet. But the hike was not hard. Sam began to look up.

"The hike up takes an hour," said Linn. "At the top we'll have lunch. Then we'll hike down."

Sam nodded.

They hiked for a bit. Sam got hot. A breeze blew his hair. It felt good.

Linn stopped. "Time for water," she said. She sat under a tree. Sam stood near her. They both had a drink.

It was cool under the trees.

"Let's keep going," said Linn. She stood up. She headed up the path. Sam walked behind her.

"This isn't so bad," said Sam. "I can do this hike."

"Good," said Linn. She climbed on a large rock. "Come up here."

Sam went to the rock. It looked hard to climb. He would have to use his hands. A tree was next to the rock. Sam grabbed the tree. It helped him get up.

"Look," said Linn. "Look at this view."

Sam looked. He saw a big valley. It was filled with trees. Lots and lots of trees. Sam felt dizzy. He grabbed the tree. He sat down on the rock.

"Isn't it great?" asked Linn.

"It's so big," said Sam. He slid off the rock. He kept his eyes down. He waited for Linn.

They hiked some more. Linn was

laughing. She loved hiking. Sam laughed too. Soon they got to the top.

"This is Blue Lake," said Linn. She smiled at Sam.

Sam looked around. They were next to a lake. It was deep blue. Trees grew around the lake. The woods were quiet. The air was still.

Linn sat by the lake. She pulled out her lunch. Sam sat by the lake. He pulled out his lunch.

Sam watched some bees. They were buzzing in flowers. Sam watched some ants.

They were carrying crumbs. Sam watched the lake. Fish were making ripples. Sam looked up at the trees. The leaves were moving.

Sam felt the wind on his face. He closed his eyes. He tilted his face up. The sunshine felt nice. He opened his eyes. Hawks were in the sky. Clouds were in the sky. The clouds were not white.

"Uh-oh," said Linn. She was looking at the clouds too. "A storm is coming. We need to leave. This won't be a summer shower. A storm will make us very wet."

She packed up. Sam did the same. A storm sounded like a bad thing.

"We'll walk fast," said Linn. She set off down the path. She was walking fast. Sam tried to keep up. But the path had many rocks. There were more clouds. They covered the sun. It was getting dark.

Then Linn gave a yell. Sam looked at her. She was on the ground. She was rubbing her ankle.

"What's wrong?" asked Sam.

"I tripped," said Linn. "My ankle hurts." Linn got up. She fell down again. "I can't walk," she said. "It hurts too much." Linn gritted her teeth.

"What can we do?" asked Sam. He had no ideas.

"I'll call Mom," said Linn. "She'll be mad. But she'll come." Linn opened her pack. She got out her phone. "Oh no!" said Linn. "Look at my phone." Linn's phone was cracked. It would not work. "Do you have your phone?" asked Linn.

"No," said Sam. "It only works on the moon."

Linn rubbed her ankle. "I know," she

said. "I know where there's a phone. In the auto-car."

"Good," said Sam. "But how will you get there?"

Linn looked at Sam. She lifted her eyebrows.

"Me?" said Sam. "You want me to go? By myself?" His face turned white. He leaned back on a tree. He slid to the ground.

9

THE STORM

"You have to go," said Linn. "Get the auto-car phone. Call my mom."

Sam gulped. Linn was right. She couldn't walk. Sam had to do it. He had to get help.

"Okay," said Sam. "I'll go."

"Go fast," said Linn. "The sky is very dark. It will rain soon."

Sam did not look up. He knew it was dark. He looked down the path.

"What if I get lost?" he asked.

"The path is easy," said Linn. "There are marks on the trees. Look for the marks. You won't get lost. Now go!"

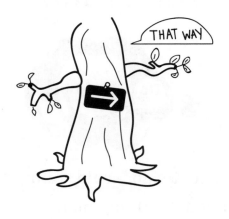

Sam jumped up. Linn was loud. Her ankle must hurt. Sam began to walk. He did not look back. He only looked down. Down the path. Down the mountain.

"Oh no!" said Sam. He felt raindrops. The rain had started. He was getting wet. But he'd been in the rain before. He'd been fine.

Sam walked on. He walked fast. He wanted to look down. But he had to look up. He had to look for the marks. He didn't want to get lost. The sky got darker. The rain got harder. Now Sam was very wet.

Then it changed. It got windy. He liked the wind up at Blue Lake. But this wind was strong. It blew leaves. It blew twigs. The leaves and twigs hit Sam.

Sam walked faster. He did not want to be scared. Rain wouldn't hurt him. Leaves wouldn't hurt him. Twigs wouldn't hurt him. He wouldn't be scared. He thought of Linn. She was in the rain too. She was in the wind. She needed help. Sam kept walking.

Flash!

Sam froze. What was that? What was that flash?

Boom! *Boom*!

Sam couldn't move. What *was* that? What was that noise?

More flashes came. And more booms. Sam knew what it was. It was a big storm. He'd seen flix of big storms. But this was different. A real storm was very different!

What could he do?

He couldn't see. The sky was dark. The rain was in his face.

He couldn't walk. The path was muddy. Twigs hit him.

He couldn't hear. The wind was loud. The thunder was louder.

He was wet and dirty. He was cold and tired. He needed to find a safe place.

← SHELTER

Sam saw a rock. It was big. It had a ledge. He could sit under it. Sam went to the rock.

He sat under the ledge. It was dry. He could wait here. Then he thought of Linn. She was not under a ledge. She was in the rain. She was in the wind. She was waiting for help. Sam got up. He would keep walking. He would get help.

Sam went slowly. He didn't want to get lost. He didn't want to trip. The hike down took a long time. But he made it. He saw the charging lot. He saw the auto-car. He punched the door code. He slid inside. He grabbed the car's phone.

10

BACK HOME

Sam walked into the living room. Linn was on the couch. Her ankle was resting. It was wrapped up. Sam looked at Linn.

"My visit is over," he said. "It's time for me to go."

Linn looked at Sam. She smiled.

"Thank you again," she said. "For hiking

to the auto-car. By yourself. In a storm. A very big storm."

"Someone had to get help," said Sam.

"You were brave," said Linn. "You could have been hurt. Big storms are bad."

"I was scared," said Sam. "I almost gave up."

THIS CLOSE
TO GIVING UP →

"You didn't," said Linn. "And I'm glad."

"Your dad was not happy," Sam said with a grin. "He had to carry you. It was a long way."

"He was mad," said Linn. "But glad I was okay."

"And Aunt Meg?" said Sam.

"Mom was mad too," said Linn. "We dripped all over the house."

"We were a mess," said Sam.

Linn laughed. Sam laughed too. He liked laughing with Linn.

Aunt Meg came in. "Are you ready?" she asked.

Sam nodded. He gave Linn a hug.

"Thanks for a great visit," said Sam. "I had fun on Earth."

Sam and Aunt Meg drove to the city. Sam looked out the window of the car. He looked at the mountain. He thought about Blue Lake. He thought about the storm.

Soon they were at the spaceport. Aunt Meg helped Sam with his bags. Then he was on the spaceship. He began the long trip home. Sam had time to think.

Finally he was back on the moon. Mom and Dad met him. Sam told them about his trip. He talked for a long time.

"It was hard," he said. "But I did it. I hiked the mountain. I had fun."

"I knew you would," said Mom.

Sam was glad to be home. He decided to visit his favorite place. He got on the rolling walkway. He went to the plant dome. It was quiet. It was cool. No biting bugs. No falling water. No blowing wind. It was very still.

Sam looked at the trees. They were small. He looked at the flowers. There were no bees. He looked at the dirt. The dirt looked clean.

What was wrong? Sam liked living on the moon. But Sam missed Earth. He missed the bugs. He missed the blue sky. He missed the big sun. He missed the weather. He missed his cousin.

Sam went back to his room. He began to type. He typed a letter to Linn.

HEY LINN,

THANKS FOR A GOOD VISIT. I
HOPE YOUR ANKLE IS BETTER.
I WAS WONDERING. COULD I
VISIT AGAIN? IN THE WINTER?
WE COULD HIKE THE MOUNTAIN
AGAIN. MAYBE THERE WILL BE
A SNOWSTORM!

SAM :)